The Unofficial

Harry Potter Spellbook

The Wand Chooses the Wizard

By Duncan Levy

E-mail: info@thinkaha.com
20660 Stevens Creek Blvd., Suite 210
Cupertino, CA 95014

Copyright © 2013 Duncan Levy

All rights reserved. No part of this book shall be reproduced, stored in a retrieval system, or transmitted by any means electronic, mechanical, photocopying, recording, or otherwise without written permission from the publisher.

Published by THiNKaha®
20660 Stevens Creek Blvd., Suite 210, Cupertino, CA 95014
http://thinkaha.com

First Printing: September 2013
Paperback ISBN: 978-1-61699-128-9 (1-61699-128-3)
eBook ISBN: 978-1-61699-129-6 (1-61699-129-1)
Place of Publication: Silicon Valley, California, USA
Paperback Library of Congress Number: 2013948425

Trademarks

All terms mentioned in this book that are known to be trademarks or service marks have been appropriately capitalized. Neither THiNKaha, nor any of its imprints, can attest to the accuracy of this information. Use of a term in this book should not be regarded as affecting the validity of any trademark or service mark.

Harry Potter is a registered trademark of Time Warner Entertainment Company.

This book is unofficial and unauthorized. It is not authorized, approved, licensed, or endorsed by J.K. Rowling, her publishers, or Time Warner Entertainment Company.

Warning and Disclaimer

Every effort has been made to make this book as complete and as accurate as possible. The information provided is on an "as is" basis. The author(s), publisher, and their agents assume no responsibility for errors or omissions. Nor do they assume liability or responsibility to any person or entity with respect to any loss or damages arising from the use of information contained herein.

Contents

The spells in this book were derived from the Harry Potter book series, film series, various Harry Potter video games, and/or the Harry Potter Trading Card Game. Asterisks have been provided next to spell names or incantations that appear in sources other than the book series.

* Spells that appear in at least one Harry Potter film.
** Spells that appear in Harry Potter video games.
*** Spells that appear in the Harry Potter Trading Card Game.

The Wand Chooses the Wizard

Introduction

This magical spell book is for all who want to express magical powers. It is divided into sections: one for each of the seven spell types (charms, healing spells, transfiguration spells, counter-spells, jinxes, hexes, and curses, including the forbidden, unforgivable curses)! You will know what kind of witch or wizard you are based on the spells you use—be safe and have fun!

Section 1

Charms

Charms alter the spell caster's targets or other capabilities and qualities. These spells can last for a really long time if they are cast by a good witch or wizard.

1

Accio (Summoning Charm): summons an object to the caster, potentially over a great distance.

2

Aguamenti (Water-Making Spell): produces a stream of water from the tip of the caster's wand.

3

Alarte Ascendare: shoots the target high into the air.

4

Alohomora (Unlocking Charm): used to unlock and open doors. It is possible to curse a door to counteract the spell.

5

Arania Exumai*: used to blast away all arachnids (spiders).

6

Arresto Momentum: slows down the movement of an object.

7

Ascendio: lifts the caster high into the air or, should he or she be underwater at the time, propels the caster to the surface.

8

Bewitched Snowballs: causes snowballs to fly at targets.

9

Bombarda: provokes small explosions. *Bombarda Maxima** is a higher level of this spell, which provokes large explosions.

10

Bubble-Head Charm: produces a bubble around the caster's head, allowing him/her to breathe while swimming.

11

Carpe Retractum (Seize and Pull Charm): produces a length of supernatural rope from the caster's wand that pulls the target to the caster.

12

Caterwauling Charm: creates a perimeter around the caster; anyone who enters this perimeter sets off a high-pitched shriek.

13

Cheering Charm: causes the target to become happy and content.

14

Cistem Aperio*: opens chests and boxes.

15

Colloportus (Locking Spell): locks doors, and presumably anything else that can be locked.

16

Colovaria (Color Change Charm): changes the color of an animal or object (e.g., the caster's hair).

17

Confundo (Confundus Charm): causes the victim to become confused and befuddled.

18

Cribbing Spell**: used to cheat on tests and papers.

19

Cushioning Charm: produces an invisible cushion on target surfaces.

20

Defodio (Gouging Spell): allows the caster to gouge large chunks out of earth or stone.

21

Deprimo: causes downward pressure on the target (e.g., a floor), which may blast a hole in the target.

22

Diffindo (Severing Charm): precisely and accurately cuts something. It can cause death or injury if used inappropriately.

23

Dissendium: opens secret passageways.

24

Duro (Hardening Charm): causes objects to harden.

25

Erecto: used to set up structures (e.g., tents).

26

Everte Statum: a dueling spell; inflicts a short burst of pain upon the target, which can make him or her stumble.

27

Expecto Patronum: creates a spirit—a Patronus—out of the caster's positive emotions. Commonly used against Dementors or Lethifolds.

28

Expelliarmus (Disarming Charm): disarms the target (e.g., disarms a wizard by causing his/her wand to fly out of reach).

29

Extinguishing Spell: puts out fires.

30

Feather-Light Charm: makes the target lightweight.

31

Flame-Freezing Charm: causes fire to become harmless. Casters will feel a tickling sensation, instead of burning.

32

Firestorm: produces a ring of fire from the caster's wand.

33

Fumos (Smokescreen Spell)**: creates a cloud of smoke from the tip of the caster's wand.

34

Fur Spell: causes fur to grow on the target.

35

Geminio: duplicates targets; creates exact replicas of targets.

36

Glacius (Freezing Spell)**: conjures ice from the tip of the caster's wand. Can extinguish fires and create ice blocks.

37

Glisseo: causes the steps of a staircase to flatten into a slide.

38

Green Sparks Spell: shoots green sparks out of the tip of the caster's wand.

39

Herbivicus***: causes flowers and plants to grow rapidly.

40

Hot-Air Charm: causes the tip of the wand to emit hot air.

41

Hover Charm: a lesser variation of the Levitation Charm; causes the target to float in mid-air.

42

Illegibilus***: renders text unreadable.

43

Immobulus: renders living things immobile.

44

Incendio (Fire-Making Spell): produces fire.

45

Intruder Charm: detects intruders and sounds an alarm.

46

*Lacarnum Inflamarae**: sends a small ball of fire from the tip of the caster's wand, usually to ignite the target's cloak on fire.

47

Legilimens (Legilimency Spell): allows the caster to delve into the mind of the victim (a.k.a. Legilimency).

48

Lumos (Wand-Lighting Charm): creates a narrow beam of light from the tip of the caster's wand.

49

Mobilicorpus: levitates and moves bodies.

50

Muffliato: fills people's ears with a buzzing sound to keep them from overhearing private conversations.

51

Obliviate (Memory Charm): erases specific memories.

52

Obscuro: causes a blindfold to appear over the target's eyes.

53

Oculus Reparo (a Mending Charm): repairs broken eyeglasses.

54

Pack: packs a trunk full of luggage.

55

Periculum: causes red sparks to shoot out of the caster's wand.

56

Point Me (Four-Point Spell): causes the caster's wand to behave as a compass and point north.

57

Prior Incantato: causes an echo of the last spell cast by a wand.

58

Quietus: causes a magically amplified voice to return back to normal.

59

Reducio (Shrinking Charm): makes an enlarged object smaller.

60

Rennervate (Reviving Spell): revives a stunned person.

61

Reparo: used to repair broken or damaged objects.

62

Repello Muggletum
(Muggle-Repelling Charm):
causes an area to be unseen
or undesirable for Muggles
to enter.

63

Rictusempra (Tickling Charm): causes an extreme tickling sensation, making the target buckle with laughter.

64

Scourgify (Scouring Charm): used to clean something.

65

Silencio: makes someone temporarily mute.

66

Slugulus Eructo (Slug-Vomiting Charm): causes the target to vomit slugs for about ten minutes.

67

Sonorus: amplifies the caster's voice.

68

Spongify (Softening Charm): softens the target area or object, making it rubbery.

69

Stupefy (Stunning Spell): stuns the victim.

70

Tarantallegra (Dancing Feet Spell): makes the target's legs dance uncontrollably.

71

Tergeo: siphons material from the target surface area (e.g., ink, dust, etc.).

72

Waddiwasi: throws small objects through the air.

73

Wingardium Leviosa (Levitation Charm): levitates and moves the target object.

Section II

Healing Spells

Healing spells improve the conditions of living
targets. If cast improperly, however, these spells
can actually harm the targets.

74

Anapneo: clears a target's blocked airway.

75

Brackium Emendo: used to heal broken bones.

76

Episkey: used to heal

minor injuries.

77

Ferula: creates a bandage and splint for broken limbs.

78

Vulnera Sanentur: causes wounds and gashes to heal and any blood to return to the target.

Section III

Transfiguration Spells

Transfiguration spells alter targets' forms or appearances. These spells are divided into four different branches: transformations (altering the physical features of targets), vanishment (causing targets to vanish), conjuration (transfigures objects from thin air), and untransfiguration (counter-spells that reverse the effects of transfigurations).

79

Avifors**: changes the target into a bird.

80

Avis (Bird-Conjuring Charm): produces a flock of birds to fly out from the caster's wand.

81

Bluebell Flames: conjures waterproof blue flames that can be carried around in a container and released.

82

Cauldron to Sieve***: transforms cauldrons or other pots and pans into sieves.

83

*Draconifors***: causes the target to change into a dragon.

84

*Ducklifors***: causes the target to change into a duck.

85

Ears to Kumquats: transforms the target's ears into kumquats for a short time.

86

Epoximise: adheres one object to another.

87

Evanesco (Vanishing Spell): vanishes the target.

88

Herbifors***: causes flowers to grow from the victim.

89

Lapifors***: causes the target to change into a rabbit.

90

Orchideous: makes a bouquet of flowers appear out of the tip of the caster's wand.

91

Piertotum Locomotor: brings inanimate objects to life (e.g., statues and suits of armor). Casters can control the target's movements.

92

Serpensortia (Snake Summons Spell): conjures a large snake to come forth from the tip of the caster's wand and attack the target.

93

Tentaclifors***: causes the target's head to change into a tentacle.

94

Vera Verto**: transforms animals into water goblets.

Section IV

Counter-Spells

Counter-spells are spells that remove, inhibit, or negate the effects of other spells.

95

Aparecium: forces invisible ink or other hidden messages to appear. Also possible to force other invisible things to appear.

96

Finite Incantatem (General Counter-Spell): counter-spell for general use.

97

Homorphus: causes a transfigured object or Animagus to return to its normal shape.

98

Protego: a shield charm that creates a barrier around the caster to deflect other spells.

99

Nox (Wand-Extinguishing Charm): puts out the light produced by *Lumos* (Wand-Lighting Charm).

100

Redactum Skullus: shrinks the target's skull. Can be used to reverse the effects of the *Engorgio Skullus* hex.

Section V

Jinxes

Jinxes are affiliated with dark magic. They are used mainly for amusement and do not majorly affect targets.

101

Cantis: causes the target to burst uncontrollably into song.

102

Cornflake Skin Spell: causes the target's skin to appear as if it has been coated in cornflakes.

103

Ebublio**: entraps the target in a large bubble that cannot be penetrated by physical force.

104

Entomorphis: induces insect-like qualities upon targets for a short period of time.

105

Flipendo (Knockback Jinx): physically repels targets or knocks away objects.

106

Impedimenta: trips, freezes, binds, or knocks back the target; does anything to keep the target away from the caster.

107

Incarcerous: ties the target with ropes.

108

Inflatus**: inflates objects.

109

Langlock: glues the targets tongue to the roof of their mouth.

110

Levicorpus: lifts the target upside-down by their ankles.

111

Melofors: encases the target's head in a pumpkin.

112

Oppugno: causes objects or individuals to attack the target.

113

Orbis**: sucks the target into the ground.

114

Relashio: causes the target to drop whatever object he or she is holding.

115

*Ventus***: shoots a strong blast of wind from the tip of the caster's wand.

Section VI

Hexes

Hexes have a strong tie to dark magic. These spells generally cause some suffering and pain to the target, but they can also be used in a defensive capacity.

116

Anteoculatia: causes the target to grow antlers.

117

Bedazzling Hex: used to disguise something.

118

Colloshoo (Stickfast Hex)***: adheres the target's shoes to the ground.

119

Densaugeo (Tooth-Growing Spell): causes the target's two front teeth to grow rapidly or regrow lost teeth.

120

Engorgio Skullus: causes the target's skull to swell in size. The counter-spell to this is *Redactum Skullus*.

121

Hurling Hex: causes the target's broom to vibrate violently and try to hurl its rider off.

122

Mutatio Skullus: mutates the target (e.g., target grows extra heads).

123

Steleus**: causes the target to sneeze violently for a short while.

124

Titilando***: tickles and weakens the target.

Section VII

Curses

Curses are the worst kind of dark magic,
intended to affect the target in the worst way
possible, usually in a way that harms
him or her physically.

125

Antonin Dolohov's Curse: a nearly lethal spell (produced by a streak of purple flame) used to create severe internal injury.

126

Babbling: causes a person to babble whenever he or she tries to speak.

127

Calvorio (Hair Loss Curse): causes the target's hair to fall out.

128

Confringo (Blasting Curse): causes anything the spell hits to explode and burst into flames.

129

Disintegration Curse: disintegrates targets.

130

Expulso: provokes a pressurized explosion with a burst of blue light.

131

Fiendfyre: a bewitched flame that seeks out targets.

132

Flagrante: causes an object to be extremely hot when touched. An object bewitched with this curse can burn flesh and other material.

133

Morsmordre: conjures the Dark Mark, the skull-and-serpent sign used by Voldemort and his Death Eaters.

134

Petrificus Totalus (Full Body-Bind Curse or Body-Freezing Spell): paralyzes the target.

135

Reducto: breaks objects.

136

Sectumsempra: causes gashes on the target, as if he or she was slashed with an invisible sword.

137

Unbreakable Vow: causes a vow that is taken between two witches or wizards to be unbreakable. If one does break the vow, he or she dies.

Section VIII

The Forbidden Section
(Unforgivable Curses)

Forbidden! Do not read!

The three most powerful, dangerous, and sinister curses in the wizarding world are known as the Unforgivable Curses. Beware of these curses if they are thrust upon you, and do not perform them on other Muggles or wizards, lest you spend your life in Azkaban!

138

Imperio: places the subject in a dream like state, in which the subject is subject to the will of the caster.

139

Crucio (Cruciatus Curse or Torture Curse): causes great pain on the target, described as a thousand hot knives being driven into the target.

140

Avada Kedavra (Killing Curse): causes an instant death to the target, accompanied by a flash of green light.

What Topic Would You Like to See a THiNKaha Book On?

Do you have an idea or topic that would do well with the THiNKaha book format? We'd like to hear from you. Please e-mail us your thoughts at info@thinkaha.com or visit http://www.thinkaha.com/contribute.

About the Author

Duncan Levy is 15 years old and has always been a huge fan of Harry Potter (he even dressed up like him for Halloween once). Duncan was inspired to write this book to give other young Harry Potter fans spells to say, rather than the standard "*Wingardium Leviosa!*"

Lightning Source UK Ltd.
Milton Keynes UK
UKOW04f1906270315

248679UK00001B/41/P